TRANSFORMERS
ROBOTS IN DISGUISE

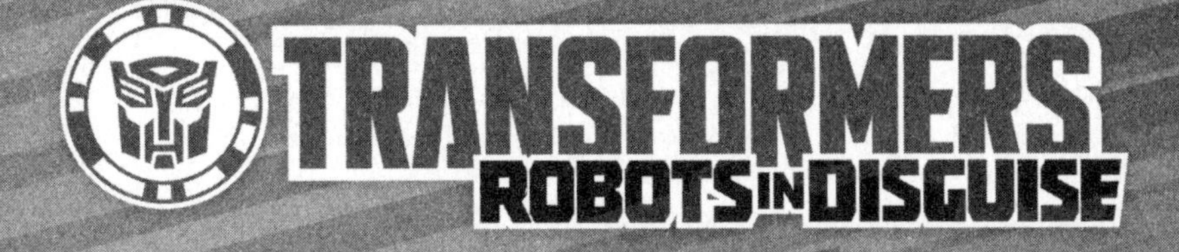

Bumblebee Versus Scuzzard

by John Sazaklis

LITTLE, BROWN AND COMPANY
New York Boston

This book is a work of fiction. Names, characters, places, and incidents are the product of the author's imagination or are used fictitiously. Any resemblance to actual events, locales, or persons, living or dead, is coincidental.

Little, Brown and Company

Hachette Book Group
1290 Avenue of the Americas, New York, NY 10104
Visit us at lb-kids.com

Little, Brown and Company is a division of Hachette Book Group, Inc.
The Little, Brown name and logo are trademarks of Hachette Book Group, Inc.

The publisher is not responsible for websites (or their content) that are not owned by the publisher.

First Edition: May 2015

Library of Congress Cataloging-in-Publication Data

Sazaklis, John.
Bumblebee versus Scuzzard / by John Sazaklis.
pages cm. — (Transformers robots in disguise)
ISBN 978-0-316-41087-8 (trade pbk.) — ISBN 978-0-316-29515-4 (ebook) — ISBN 978-0-316-29375-4 (library edition ebook)
I. Title.
PZ7.S27587Bum 2015
[Fic]—dc23

2014046763

10 9 8 7 6 5 4 3 2 1

RRD-C

Printed in the United States of America

Licensed By:

Bumblebee

Sideswipe
Strongarm

Grimlock
Scuzzard

Chapter 1

"Stop in your tracks, Decepticon!" shouts Bumblebee. "You're under arrest!"

The Autobot leader blasts his plasma cannon. The rapidly moving target leaps from side to side then somersaults over the Cybertronian lieutenant, landing behind him. The agile adversary shoves Bumblebee to the ground.

"Is that the best you got, law-bot?" taunts a familiar voice.

It is Bumblebee's teammate: the youthful, energetic, and rebellious Sideswipe.

He scowls at Bumblebee and yells, "You're scrap metal!"

Sideswipe then smiles, extends his arm, and helps his sparring partner off the ground.

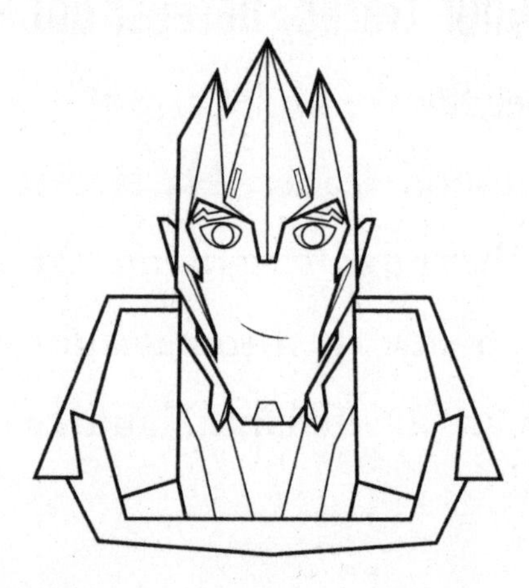

"Pretty impressive," Bumblebee says. "You've got some nice moves, but the tough-bot attitude might be a bit over the top, don't you think?"

The young Autobot laughs. "You got to be a tough-bot if you want to intimidate those Decepticons, Bee."

"Thanks for the advice," Bumblebee replies. "Who's next?"

The Autobot leader scans the scrapyard that currently serves as their headquarters and training area.

Located on the outskirts of Crown City on planet Earth, the scrapyard belongs to a pair of humans: Denny Clay and his son, Russell. The Clays have befriended Bumblebee and his robot team and sometimes help them on their mission to track down and capture a number of Decepticon fugitives from the planet Cybertron.

“It is my turn, sir,” calls out Strongarm. The young cadet dutifully strides over to the center of the training area.

Back on Cybertron, Strongarm was a member of the police force serving under Lieutenant Bumblebee. Now she helps serve and protect anyone or anything that may come to harm at the hands of the Autobots’ evil enemies on Earth.

“Let’s see if your moves are as good as mine,” Sideswipe says to her. “Not everyone gets the best of Bee. But *I* did!”

“Show some respect, Sideswipe,” replies Strongarm. “You may have advanced ‘street smarts' back home, but you're no intellitron. Bumblebee is your commanding officer, and you should treat him as such!"

"You're right," snaps Sideswipe. "So I only have to listen to *him*. Not you!"

"Fine," huffs the police-bot. "Who says I want to waste nanocycles talking to *you* anyway?" Strongarm retorts. "I'd have to use smaller words and talk... very... slowly."

"Enough!" Bumblebee says, exasperated. "We are all on the *same* team, whether we like to admit it or not. The real foes are out there and we need to be prepared. Something terrible is on the horizon, and by the AllSpark, I sure hope we can handle it!"

"Yes, sir," Strongarm says. "Let's continue training."

"Where are Grimlock and Drift?" Sideswipe asks.

Grimlock is a dinobot and former Decepticon who defected to the Autobots, and Drift is an honorable bounty hunter. They're also part of Bumblebee's ragtag team.

"Drift has a free pass from today's training," Bumblebee replies. "He took the Groundbridge to an area with an allegedly high concentration of Energon. You know how he likes his solo missions."

"Yeah, Drift sure is a real-deal tough-bot," Sideswipe says. "Glad he's on our side."

Bumblebee chuckles. "I asked him to recon and report back," the leader says. "If there is Energon out there, we'll travel to the location and harvest the power source right away."

"Excellent," Strongarm cheers. "Another mission!"

"I totally understand your enthusiasm, Strongarm," Bumblebee replies. "Things have been a little quiet around here."

"Yeah, quiet until the storm hits," Sideswipe says, slamming his fist into his palm. "I'm ready for whatever the Decepticons got!"

"I have a feeling the Decepticons may be

after something as big and as powerful as the AllSpark."

Strongarm gasps. "But, sir, harnessing that kind of power could bring about unimaginable destruction!"

Bumblebee nods grimly.

Sideswipe breaks the uncomfortable silence and tries to lighten the mood. "Speaking of destruction, what's Grimlock up to?"

"He's recharging on top of a pile of old cars," a voice answers.

The Autobots turn to see Russell, their twelve-year-old human friend. "Grimlock found a nice sunny spot, and he's lying in it like a big lizard."

"Hey, Russell," Bumblebee says. "What's up?"

"Shouldn't you be at lob-ball practice?" asks Sideswipe.

Russell chuckles. "Here on Earth, it's called football."

"Oh, right," Sideswipe says, trying to remember the word. "Foot. Ball."

"We're on spring break from school," Russell continues.

"Spring break?" Strongarm asks, puzzled.

"Yeah."

Suddenly, Fixit rolls into the training area from behind a dented billboard.

"Who has a spring break?" Fixit asks. "It's about time! I've been itching to repaint... repeat... repair something."

The multitasking mini-con was pilot of the prison transport ship *Alchemor*—the same ship that crashed to Earth and let loose the Decepticon criminals aboard. Now he rounds out the rest of Team Bee as the resident handy-bot.

After the crash, Fixit developed a minor stutter, but he manages to correct his vocabulary with a quick check.

The mini-con weaves in and out between the legs of the Autobots, twitching his digits excitedly.

"No one had anything break," Bumblebee says, looking himself over. "As far as I can tell."

Russell laughs. "Spring break is another term for taking a vacation from school."

"What's a vacation?" Strongarm asks.

"It's time off," Sideswipe replies. "Like an extended holiday."

Strongarm's optics open wide with surprise. "Who would want to take time off from school?"

"Not Miss Perfect Attendance, I'm sure," Sideswipe retorts.

"Every single cycle!" Strongarm announces proudly.

"Really? I'm impressed, cadet," Bumblebee says. "That's an excellent record!"

"I know!" Strongarm beams.

Sideswipe rolls his optic sensors.

"Anyway," Russell interrupts. "My friends Hank and Butch are going away with their families for the next week and, well, I'm kind of stuck here, where nothing exciting has happened in *ages*."

The boy kicks a rock and sits on an overturned shopping cart.

"That's not so bad," Fixit replies. "I'm stumped . . . stunned . . . stuck here all the time when all the other bots are out on missions or when they play games together."

"Every team member's duty is very important," Bumblebee explains. "Especially yours, Fixit."

Sideswipe sighs. "All right. There's only so much sappy goodness this bot can take before he gets brain rust."

He walks over and crouches near the mini-con.

"So, you *really* wanna play lob-ball with us? You got it!"

With a loud whistle, the red robot wakes up Grimlock.

"Big G!" Sideswipe hollers. "We're playing lob-ball with Fixit. Go long!

"Finally!" Grimlock exclaims as he stretches his limbs. "Something to do that involves some action!"

Fixit rubs his digits together with anticipation and excitement.

"Excellent. What's my position?"

Sideswipe smirks and picks up the mini-con.

"Ball," he says.

Then, in one deft movement, he hurls Fixit through the air straight at Grimlock.

"AAAAAAAAAH!" screams the mini-con as he becomes a tiny dot against the sky.

Bumblebee sighs and hangs his head.

"When I said we need to focus on working as a team, this is not what I had in mind."

Chapter 2

Grimlock jumps off the pile of cars and dashes into action. Shifting into his bot mode, he grabs an old metal bathtub and scrunches it onto his head.

With his makeshift helmet secured, the dinobot rushes toward Fixit, all the while giving a running commentary.

"This is it, ladies and gentlebots! Only mere nanocycles left in the game. Cybertron Lob-ball Legend Gridlock Grimlock sprints to catch the final pass. Will it be the winning play? Keep your optics open. You won't want to miss a thing!"

"Gridlock! Grimlock! Gridlock! Grimlock!" chants Sideswipe.

Grimlock catches Fixit, pulls him into his chest, pivots, and charges in the opposite direction. When he reaches the end of the scrapyard, he hoists Fixit high into the air.

"Grimlock wins the game for Team Bee! The crowd goes wild!"

Sideswipe turns on his car radio speakers and blasts a bass-heavy techno sports jam.

"Go, Grimlock, it's your botday!" he sings, while dancing to the beat.

Caught up in the excitement, Grimlock moves to spike Fixit into the ground as if he were a real football!

"Grimlock, *no*!" Strongarm shouts.

Quick as a flash, she and Bumblebee shift into their vehicle modes and rush to the rescue.

They corner Grimlock just as he spikes the mini-con. Bumblebee's tires screech and squeal and kick up dirt as he pulls a 180-degree turn. The yellow sports car pops his trunk, and Fixit lands safely inside.

Bumblebee then changes back into bot mode and cradles the mini-con.

Fixit's gears are rattling. "I think that's enough feet...feed...fieldwork for one day. Thanks."

As Bumblebee readies himself to scold Grimlock, Sideswipe blindsides him and snatches Fixit from his arms.

"INTERCEPTION!" shouts Sideswipe, and he sprints away toward the other end of the yard.

Grimlock bounds after him.

Bumblebee throws up his hands and looks at the sky. When he feels troubled, he seeks guidance from his fallen hero, Optimus Prime.

"Optimus, if you can hear me, please give me a sign. Anything that will—aha!"

A shiny object glints in the sunlight, catching Bumblebee's attention.

For a moment, the Autobot sees the reflection of Optimus Prime, but it is gone as soon as it appeared.

It is that same object that gives Bumblebee an idea. Shifting into vehicle mode, he speeds past the other Autobots and reaches the end of the scrapyard first. He switches back and climbs inside a truck with a hydraulic magnet attached. Bumblebee pulls down on a large lever and the machine whirs to life. The hydraulic arm drops toward the ground—at the same exact moment that Grimlock and Sideswipe race by underneath!

CLANG!

CLANG!

The robots are yanked off their feet and right onto the magnet.

"AAH!" they shout.

Sideswipe freaks out and drops Fixit, but Strongarm is there to catch him.

The mini-con's optic sensors are swirling wildly. He is seeing double.

"Strongarm, how long have you had a sitter . . . a sitar . . . a sister?" he asks. "Are you twigs . . . twits . . . twins? She looks just like you! Pleasure to meet you, my dear!"

Fixit bows his head and passes out.

"Hey, what's the big idea?" Sideswipe hollers.

"Game over," Bumblebee says sternly.

Grimlock looks down and sees his feet dangling high above the yard.

"I can fly!" he cheers.

Bumblebee pulls the lever again, deactivating the magnet, and releases his fellow Autobots onto the ground below.

CRASH!

Suddenly, Denny Clay comes running into the scrapyard. He is flustered and gasping for breath.

"Dad, is everything okay?" Russell asks.

"You'll never guess what happened!" Denny blurts out.

"What is it?"

"It's something that's going to change our lives forever!"

Russell looks at the robots and says, "What could possibly change our lives *more* than our new houseguests?"

"It's not kittens, is it?" Grimlock asks warily.

The dinobot has an incredible fear of cats but tries not to let it show.

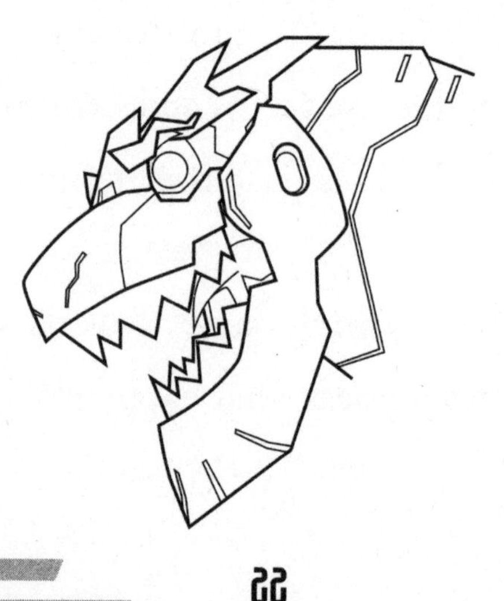

"I think I hear Drift calling me. I'll go see what he wants."

The dinobot runs away to the other side of the scrapyard, much to the bewilderment of his teammates.

Denny sits down to catch his breath. He is huffing and puffing and wheezing.

A revived Fixit rolls over and scans him.

"I'm not familiar with organic biology, but it appears that Denny Clay is running on fumes. Does he need more fuel? I have my grandbot's home remedy right here in the holo-scroll!"

Fixit rolls away into the command center.

After what seems like an eternity for the anxious group, Denny finally catches his breath and says, "An old friend of mine called up to say he's got two amazing items for sale. You'll never guess! Okay, I'll tell you. Vintage pinball machines!"

Russell, disappointed, slumps his shoulders. "Oh. More junk."

"Hey, these things are *super*rare!" Denny says excitedly. "Not exactly in working order, but it'll give us something to do together when we repair them."

"Pardon us for asking," Bumblebee interrupts, "but what are pinball machines. Are they good or bad?"

"Do they shoot pins?" Strongarm asks.

"Ha, no!" Denny says with a laugh. "They're old-fashioned coin-operated arcade games."

"Oooh, games!" Sideswipe says.

"Don't get too excited," Russell responds.

"They're ancient history. Just like everything else in this place."

Denny tries to cheer up his son. "Come on, Rusty. We'll take a little road trip together. It'll be a blast and a half! Things seem to be quiet here."

"Your father is right," Bumblebee says. "I'm confident we can manage for a while without you. Go and enjoy yourselves."

"Fine," Russell says. Then he whispers to Sideswipe. "Call us back immediately if something exciting happens, so I don't die of boredom."

"You got it, dude."

As Denny and Russell head inside to prepare for their trip, the Autobots disperse throughout the yard.

Grimlock returns with a brave face. "Hey, I don't think that was Drift calling me after all!" he says with a chuckle.

Seeing that he is alone, a wave of panic grips the dinobot.

"Oh no!" He gulps. "It *was* kittens!"

Chapter 3

"All aboard!" Denny says as he climbs into his pickup truck.

Russell climbs into the passenger seat and buckles himself in. His father is elated.

"I can't wait to get my hands on those fantastic fixer-uppers!"

"So, where are we headed exactly?"

"My old high school buddy Doug Castillo owns an arcade near the amusement park. Doug's Den is the name, and he's got *all* the old-school video games. I always wanted to take you there when you were younger but never got the chance."

As Denny loses himself in a wave of nostalgia, Russell falls silent and stares out the window. It's true his father was not around much when he was growing up. Now, with his mom traveling in Europe, Russell is spending a lot more time with his dad.

It was not long after Russell moved to the scrapyard, or, as his father calls it, the "vintage salvage depot for the discriminating nostalgist," that the Autobots literally crash-landed into their lives.

Russell watches the trees whiz by and wonders how vast the universe must be if alien robots really exist on other planets. Especially when these robots are sentient beings with the ability to reconfigure their alien anatomy into that of vehicles or animals while battling one another right outside his very home.

The pickup continues over the bridge leading into the city. Denny rolls down the windows and turns on the radio. A summer-like beach-rock tune fills the air.

Denny sighs happily. "It's good to get away!"

Meanwhile, underneath the bridge in a murky marsh, a large metallic object glints in the sun. Part of it is submerged in water and most of the exterior is damaged.

When the *Alchemor* crashed to Earth, a number of prison cells known as stasis pods were scattered across the surrounding area.

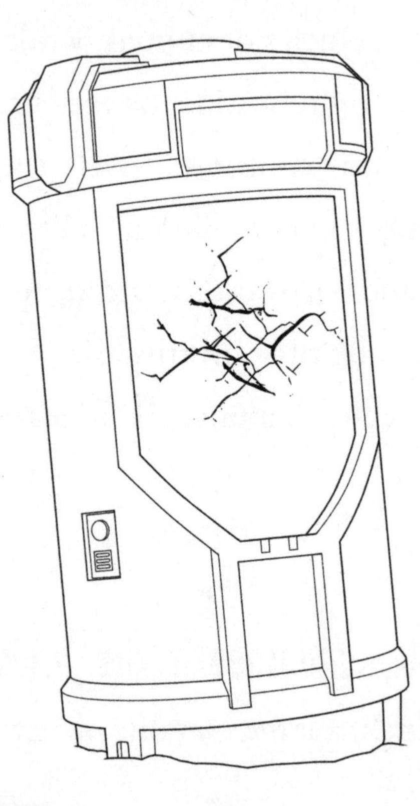

Those pods housed Cybertron's most violent criminals—Decepticons.

Unfortunately, some of them had escaped their pods, and it is Bumblebee's mission to round up the rogues.

This particular pod starts to shift and rattle as the prisoner stirs within.

CRACK.

CRACK.

CRACK.

A sharp, pointed beak pecks at the surface as if hatching an egg until it finally breaks through the stasis pod.

SKRAAAACK!

An oversized, rust-colored vulturish Decepticon emerges!

Stretching his long neck and long wings,

the creature steps, blinking, into the sun. It scours the terrain for food.

"I HUNGER!" he screeches.

His raspy, grainy voice startles a nearby bullfrog, which leaps into the water.

Following the movement, the Decepticon stabs at the water with his beak and pulls out a soggy rubber boot.

"Meh!" he exclaims in disgust and flings it aside. "What is this? Where *am* I?" He turns his head from side to side, observing his surroundings.

"This is not Cybertron. We must have landed on another, far inferior planet."

Then he spots a discarded tin can. "Is that the best sustenance this ragged rock has to offer?" he squawks.

He pinches the can with his beak and swallows it in one gulp.

Suddenly, the Decepticon feels a wonderful sensation. His body ripples with energy. It grows bigger and more menacing.

"Hmm, this rock may have something to offer me after all!"

Russell and his father finally arrive at the amusement park and drive around to where Doug's Den is located.

A man with glasses and a ponytail is waiting for them with a big grin on his face. Russell guesses that it is Doug.

"Denny, you ol' sea dog!" Doug hollers

as Russell and his dad exit the pickup. He squeezes Denny in a bear hug that lifts him off the ground.

"Dougie, you haven't changed a bit. I want you to meet my son, Rusty."

The boy shakes Doug's hand and says, "It's Russell, actually."

"And I'm Doug," the man says with a wink. "Come on in, I'll show you around!"

Russell and his father walk through the arcade, looking at all the classic video games. There is one where a yellow circle with a mouth eats white dots while running from multicolored ghosts. Another one stars a short plumber with a mustache that has to save a princess.

"*Wow!* This is awesome!" Denny gushes. "What do you think, Rusty?"

"I think it's cool... if not a little *old*."

"Russell, apologize!" his father scolds.

Doug laughs. "No offense taken. The boy's right. Kids today have portable, digital, highly advanced technology in the palm of their hands. Why would they waste their time with these clunky old dinosaurs?"

"You don't need to tell *me* about clunky dinosaurs," Denny says. He looks at Russell with a gleam in his eye. Russell smiles knowingly.

"I might as well shut this place down or turn it into a museum," Doug continues. "I'll charge people to come in and hear me say,

'The first coin-operated pinball machine was introduced in 1931.'"

Denny brightens. "And speaking of pinball machines..."

"Oh, yes! Right this way."

The group circles around back to the loading dock, where two time-ravaged pinball machines stand wrapped in plastic.

Russell can see the intricate illustrations painted on the back panels of each game. They are of a grizzled adventurer wearing a leather jacket and brown fedora. In one, he is riding a horse into the mouth of a cave shaped like a skull. In the other, he swings on a rope over a pit of cobras surrounded by flames.

Hmm, maybe these things aren't so boring after all, Russell thinks.

About half an hour later, after loading their truck and bidding Doug farewell, the duo is back on the road again.

"I can't wait to tinker with them," Denny says. "Maybe even put some of that Autobot tech in 'em. Make 'em outta this world!"

Rusty smiles. That turned out to be a fun little adventure after all.

When they reach the bridge, Denny slams on the brakes.

There appears to be a traffic jam, with several bystanders looking over the side of the bridge.

Suddenly, a screeching creature swoops up into the air.

"Is that a hawk?" Russell asks.

"It looks more like a vulture," Denny says,

puzzled. "We don't have many in these parts, though."

Just as suddenly, the winged beast dives and lands on the hood of the pickup, denting it under his massive weight.

CRUNCH!

Denny and Russell see the Decepticon logo on the vulture's gleaming metallic hide.

"Wish we had some Autobot tech with us right now!" Russell yells.

Chapter 4

SCREEEEEECH!

The sound of metal scraping metal is ear piercing as the Decepticon digs his claws into the hood of Denny's pickup truck.

"A prisoner has escaped!" Russell cries.

"Rusty, look out!" shouts Denny.

The vulture pecks at the glass with his giant

beak. Thin cracks creep across the windshield in a spiderweb pattern.

"We gotta call Bumblebee!" yells Russell.

"First, we gotta get this thing away from the people," replies Denny. He wrenches the wheel to the left, causing the pickup to go off the road and into the woods.

The Decepticon hisses in surprise and digs his talons in deeper to maintain a grip on the hood. Then he glares at Denny.

"We're taking the scenic route, you big buzzard," Denny says.

Rusty fumbles for the CB radio on the truck's dashboard. Once he pries it loose, he clicks on the receiver to open a connection.

The pickup's tires bump along the uneven

terrain, jostling Russell. He drops the radio, and it slides under his seat.

Denny shouts a warning as the Decepticon rears his head back for another attack. “Get down and cover your head!”

The vulture stabs at the glass again, this time penetrating it with his beak.

SHUNK!

“AAAH!”

Denny screams and reflexively turns on the windshield wipers. They begin swishing from side to side, momentarily hypnotizing the rampaging robot.

Screeching with annoyance, the Decepticon chomps down and rips them off. He chews them but finds them unsatisfactory.

"BLEH!" he yells, spitting them out. Then he turns to attack again. The windshield will not withstand another hit.

Denny uses his wits and—in a last-ditch effort—squirts the bad birdbot with wiper fluid.

SQUIRRRT!

The liquid coats the vulture's face, blinding him. Flailing his wings, he loses balance and lurches backward.

Denny cuts the wheel one more time,

causing the truck to swerve in a complete circle. The Decepticon tumbles off the hood, claws at the air, and slams into a nearby tree trunk.

BAM!

Unfortunately, one of the pinball machines is jarred loose and falls out and onto the ground. The glass display shatters into a million pieces. The metal gears and ball bearings roll over the grass, glinting and shimmering under the sun.

This catches the vulture's attention, and he descends upon the arcade game, rending it apart. The priceless pinball machine is now nothing more than a worthless chew toy.

"Oh, man!" Denny laments, looking over his shoulder.

Without a moment to lose, he slams on the gas and the pickup truck speeds off toward the scrapyard.

Russell finally gets his hands on the CB radio and tries to contact the command center.

"There's no answer, Dad," he says.

Denny gulps and tries not to look worried in front of his son. He wipes the sweat off his brow with the back of his hand.

"Do you think our friends are in trouble?" Russell asks.

"Only one way to find out," replies Denny. "We're almost there."

Father and son ride the rest of the way in silence, both wondering what will be the outcome of this Decepticon disaster.

Chapter 5

When Russell and Denny arrive, they jump out of the truck and rush into the scrapyard, only to find it eerily quiet.

"Where is everyone?" Russell asks.

"Let's hope they didn't get carried away," Denny says.

"Dad!" Russell says.

With his father, the young boy runs up and down the aisles of piled junk calling out the names of their friends.

Suddenly, there is a loud crash and crunching of metal followed by painful grunts and sounds of a struggle.

"Oh no!" Russell exclaims. "That sounds like trouble to me!"

The humans sprint through the mazelike scrapyard until they discover the source of the commotion.

There, in a clearing between the busted lawn mowers and a broken tractor, is an Autobot pileup.

Sideswipe is sprawled out on the bottom.

Lying on top of him are Bumblebee, then Strongarm, and finally Grimlock.

They look exhausted and defeated. Russell notices that the robots are barely moving.

"Our friends picked the wrong time to shut down," Denny says. "Now what are we going to do?"

Rusty cups his hands around his mouth and shouts. "HELP!"

The Autobots stir and turn toward the boy.

"Welcome back!" Sideswipe says cheerily from the bottom of the pile.

The robots climb off one another and help Sideswipe to his feet. Clutched close to his chest is a large concrete wrecking ball.

"We finally played a proper game of

lob-ball," he says. "And this ball is *much* better than Fixit!"

"I concur," says the mini-con, scurrying out from behind a trash can.

"See?" Sideswipe says. "Now I can do *this*!"

With one swift motion, he spikes the wrecking ball into the ground, lifting a cloud of dust and debris.

Bumblebee walks over and asks, "How was your trip?"

"Terrible!" Russell exclaims. "While you guys were running around, *we* were running for our lives!"

"What happened?" Strongarm asks.

"We were attacked by a flying Decepticon," Denny tells the group.

Stunned, the Autobots look at one another.

Without a moment to lose, they shift into their vehicle modes.

Bumblebee becomes a sleek yellow sports car and scoops up Denny into his cab.

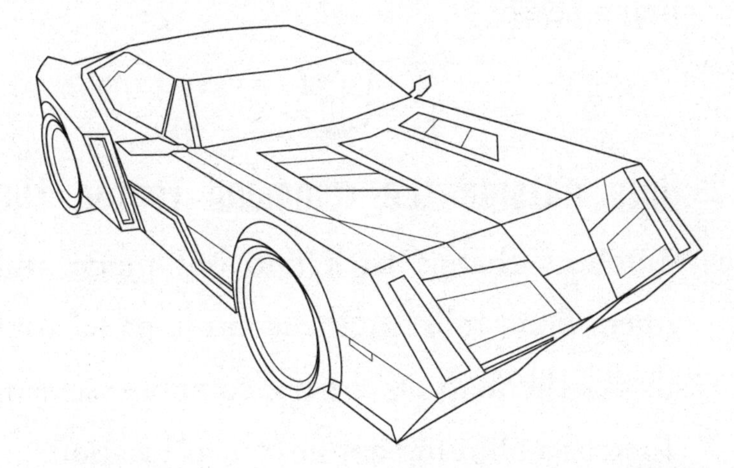

Sideswipe has the flashier and shinier appearance of a red sports car and takes Russell in tow.

Strongarm prides herself in her identity as a police sport-utility vehicle.

Fixit and Grimlock follow along in their bot modes because they do not have secret vehicle appearances to change into.

Together they all zoom back to the command center.

Once outside the command center, the Autobots change back into bot mode and enter. Fixit rolls to the control panel and checks the map on the big computer screen. There is a blinking dot near their location.

"It would appear that there is another Decepticon on the loon . . . loop . . . loose," he says.

"You're not far off," Denny replies. "This creature *was* birdlike."

"He has razor-sharp claws and a beak and wings!" Rusty adds. "He almost made a meal out of the pickup!"

Fixit clacks away on the keyboard, calling up all known flying Decepticons on the *Alchemor*'s manifest. A few seconds later, several images appear on the holo-scroll.

Rusty and Denny point at their assailant simultaneously.

"That one!" they shout.

"His name is Scuzzard," Bumblebee reads. "And he is a Scavengebot. His abilities are similar to those of a Chompozoid."

"Our enemy Underbite is a Chompozoid, remember?" Strongarm adds. "When these Decepticons consume metal, it supercharges their bodies until they become unstoppable."

"Scavengebots have the compulsion to rend everything apart before they consume it. Most of them are pretty harmless and feast on scrap metal," explains Bumblebee. "Not Scuzzard, though."

"Hmm, I seem to remember his case," Strongarm says. "He was arrested for laying waste to a good part of Kaon's industrial area. It took an entire squadron of the capital's police force to detain and contain him!"

Denny spoke up. "This creature was about to destroy the bridge before he set his sights on us. Made a meal out of one of my poor pinball machines, too."

"So what's the plan, sir?" Strongarm asks.

"Good question," Bumblebee replies. "We need to lure the predator away from civilians, get him into a secluded area, and subdue him as quickly as possible."

"Finally!" Sideswipe says. "Just what I needed to flex my pistons!"

Bumblebee smiles. "You've given me an idea, Sideswipe. We'll send *you* out as a decoy."

"Wait, what?" replies the young Autobot. "That is a *bad* idea."

"Not really," adds Strongarm. "You're red,

shiny, and quick to catch attention. Perfect bait!"

"And you're fast," concludes Bumblebee.

Sideswipe tries to protest, but he agrees with everything his teammates have said.

"You're right," he says. "I make Decepticon hunting look *good*."

The hotshot Autobot admires his own reflection in the mirror of an old vanity nearby.

Strongarm aims her blaster and pulverizes the piece of furniture.

"Eek!" Grimlock shrieks. "That's seven cycles of bad luck!"

"Get *over* yourself," Strongarm says to Sideswipe.

"*You* get over *your*self!" Sideswipe retorts.

"Let's get this mission over with, please," Bumblebee interrupts. Then he doles out orders to the rest of the team. "Fixit, send us Scuzzard's coordinates."

As the mini-con complies, Russell and Denny consult the map.

"Hmm, that buzzardbot seems to have flown into town and is circling the area above my buddy's arcade," Denny observes.

"You have to move fast before he attacks!" Russell says.

"There's a mile of deserted road in the forest leading back here," Denny tells Bumblebee. "It's a longer route, but you can avoid the bridge and being seen by humans."

"Thank you," Bumblebee says. Then he turns to Sideswipe.

"You will get Scuzzard's attention and lure him back to the deserted road. Strongarm and I will be waiting to form a triangulation and trap him with our neo-forges."

"What about me?" asks Grimlock.

"You will stay here. These Decepticons are unpredictable. If any more of them appear, we will need you as one of our last defenses here at the base."

Forlorn, Grimlock hangs his head.

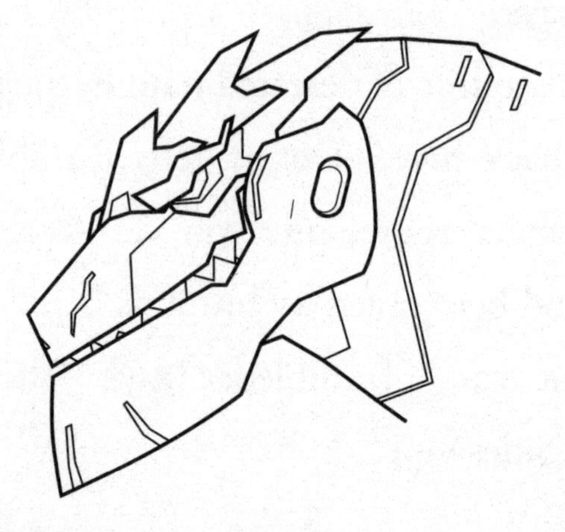

"Okay, team," says Bumblebee. "Let's cruise down to bruisetown!"

The Autobots stand still and stare at their leader. His attempts at a trademark rallying cry have been less than successful since they've arrived on Earth.

Sideswipe smiles. "How 'bout we just rock and roll?"

Bumblebee sighs. "Yeah, we can do that, too."

Quick as a flash, Sideswipe, Strongarm, and Bumblebee shift into vehicle mode and zoom out of the scrapyard.

Speeding through the forest, the Autobots trace Russell and Denny's trail to the old arcade. Their radar screens blip faster and louder, indicating that the Decepticon is near.

Bumblebee and Strongarm fall back and disappear behind a thicket of trees. They lie in wait, and Sideswipe puts his part of the plan into action.

In the distance, the red sports car sees a dark shape in the sky circling Doug's Den. At that moment, the back door opens and Doug himself exits the building. He is carrying a trash can, which he empties into a shiny metal Dumpster. Then he reenters the arcade.

Once the coast is clear, Scuzzard dives straight down and lands on the Dumpster, scattering garbage everywhere. He folds his massive wings behind him and proceeds to take giant bites out of the metal with his beak.

Sideswipe watches as the Decepticon devours the Dumpster. With each chomp, a light shimmers over his body, and Scuzzard grows larger in size. He squawks with evil glee and continues his meal.

From across the street, the Autobot steels himself and drives into the empty parking lot of the arcade.

He revs his engine.

VROOOM! VROOOM!

Scuzzard is so engrossed, he does not notice the vehicle behind him.

Exasperated, Sideswipe honks his horn impatiently, startling the escaped convict.

BEEEEEEEEEP!

Scuzzard chokes and coughs up bits of chewed metal, which land and skitter away on the asphalt.

"ACK!" He gasps. "Can't a bot eat in peace? I haven't had a decent meal in five cycles!"

Sideswipe honks again.

BEEEEEEEEEP!

Scuzzard whirls around to find a fire-engine red sports car made of delicious metal. "Well, well," he says, cocking his head. "Now, *that* looks like a decent meal!" Scuzzard stretches his wings and leaps toward Sideswipe.

The Autobot peels back in reverse, kicking up gravel, and pulls a 180-degree turn. Then he burns rubber right out of the parking lot.

"Sideswipe to Team Bee," the hero calls into his radio. "The birdbot has flown the coop . . . and he's coming right at me!"

"Perfect," Bumblebee responds. "Now lead him to us!"

Scuzzard watches as his savory snack races away.

"I love it when they play hard to eat," he says to himself.

The Decepticon soars high into the air for an aerial view of Sideswipe. Once the Autobot is in his sights, Scuzzard swoops down to attack.

"It's dinnertime!"

Chapter 6

Sideswipe senses his attacker gaining on him, and he barrels off the main highway and into the nearby forest. This causes Scuzzard to lose his visual on the Autobot.

The Decepticon slows his descent and peers through the treetops. Every couple of seconds, Sideswipe's red body becomes visible amid the lush green foliage.

"These peculiar organic objects may provide you temporary cover, my tender morsel, but your brightness betrays you," Scuzzard says aloud. "You're as good as digested!"

Scuzzard dives into the trees in one swift motion. His blunt body savagely rips its way through the thick branches, tearing them apart as if they were made of paper.

Sideswipe is inches away from the razor-sharp talons of his airborne adversary. He slams on the brakes and comes to a screeching halt. Scuzzard passes right over him, grazing the Autobot with his claws.

"Hey, watch the paint job, you big slag-heap!" Sideswipe shouts.

Scuzzard is slightly taken aback by the talking vehicle.

"Hmm, looks like my next meal is more than meets the eye," he says, squinting.

Sideswipe drives into a clearing and switches into his bot mode.

"If there's even the tiniest scratch on me, you'll be eating liquid fuel for a cycle!"

"It appears there's an Autobot among us," the Decepticon hisses.

Scuzzard lands and folds his wings. Then he extends to his full height, towering over Sideswipe.

The young hero had not realized how much bigger the Decepticon was up close. From afar, he seemed like a puny and easy enough challenge.

"Mama-bot told me not to play with my food, but tearing you apart is going to be *fun*!" Scuzzard gloats.

He slowly advances toward Sideswipe. The hotheaded Autobot is starting to lose his cool. He whispers into his communicator.

"Hey, guys? I could really use some backup right about now."

"We're trying to find you," Bumblebee responds.

Strongarm pipes in. "If you had stayed on course and met at the rendezvous point, this wouldn't be an issue."

Sideswipe quickly glances around. Strongarm is right. He is in the wrong part of the woods. He must have lost his way trying to outrun the Decepticon. Scuzzard sharpens his bladed fingertips against one another. The metal sparks and shrieks, causing Sideswipe to wince.

"This will not be quick, Autobot," rasps the criminal.

"Quick is what I do best," Sideswipe replies, and turns to hightail it out of the clearing.

Just as quickly, Scuzzard pounces. He hits the Autobot square in the back, pinning him to the ground. Sinking into the dirt, Sideswipe struggles under the massive weight of the Decepticon.

"You're barely an appetizer!" Scuzzard says.

"You don't wanna to eat me," grunts Sideswipe. "I'll just get stuck in your intake valve."

"On the contrary," replies Scuzzard. "Since

my incarceration, I've built up quite an appetite."

"Then eat this!" Sideswipe yells.

He grabs a fistful of mud and hurls it at Scuzzard's face.

The Decepticon reels back.

Sideswipe rolls onto his feet.

"What is this?" spits Scuzzard. "It's vile!"

Thinking quickly, Sideswipe says, "It's a very toxic and poisonous Earth element. It will instantly deactivate you!"

Scuzzard falls to his knees and chokes.

"Curse you, Autobot!" he gasps.

Sideswipe can't believe his good fortune.

The bigger they are, the dumber they are, he thinks.

Quickly shifting into his vehicle form, Sideswipe drives farther into the forest to look for his friends.

A yellow blur blows right past him and Sideswipe swerves to follow. “Bumblebee!” he cries.

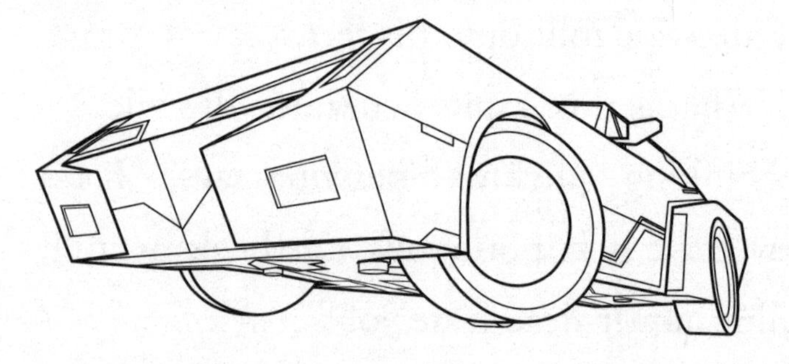

The team leader reverses and idles up next to the sports car.

Strongarm, in her police cruiser form, rolls up seconds later.

“What is the status report?” she asks.

"And where is the Decepticon?" adds Bumblebee.

As Sideswipe prepares to tell his tale, a dark shadow swoops by overhead.

SCREEECH!

"Heads up!" Strongarm warns.

The vulturish Decepticon descends upon the red sports car, landing on the roof.

"Nice try, slick," Scuzzard says, folding his wings. "You had me going for a nanocycle, but I'm still active. Only now, I'm angry!"

He rakes his sharp talons across the young hero, causing Sideswipe to yelp in pain.

Bumblebee and Strongarm surround Side-swipe and Scuzzard.

"Let me guess," the villain says. "More Autobots in disguise?"

"You got that right, criminal!" Strongarm shouts.

She shifts into her bot mode, as does Bumblebee.

"You are under arrest by order of the Cybertronian Police Force!" he says.

"*Ha!*" rasps Scuzzard. "Don't make me laugh, law-bot. We're not on Cybertron anymore!"

Scuzzard lunges at the heroes, extending his bladed wings. Bumblebee and Strongarm backflip with ease out of the criminal's razor-sharp reach. The Decepticon lands with a thud.

With his body and pride wounded, Sideswipe drives behind a row of trees and hides. He changes back into bot mode.

Bumblebee and Strongarm are ready for battle. They produce their plasma cannons and aim them at the Decepticon.

"Fire!" Bumblebee commands.

CHOOM! CHOOM!

The laser beams whiz past the vulture. He evades the blasts by soaring into the air.

"I'm just as equipped as you are," says Scuzzard as he fires a series of bladed missiles from his wings.

FWIP! FWIP! FWIP!

"Aerial assault!" Strongarm cries.

The knifelike projectiles slice through the air, stabbing everything in their path.

Bumblebee and Strongarm run for cover, but one of the bladed darts nicks Bumblebee on the leg. He stumbles and falls.

"ARGH!"

Strongarm aims her blaster from behind a tree and fires at the birdbot.

ZAP!

The energy burst catches Scuzzard square in the chest.

"Direct hit!" she cheers.

As Scuzzard falls back, he unleashes another volley of missiles.

Strongarm dives for cover as the projectiles splinter the trunk above her head. The last bladed dart bounces off her shoulder.

"Yowch!"

She spins around, reeling from the hit, and lands on her back.

Scuzzard reconfigures himself into his

large, intimidating robot form and saunters over.

He picks Strongarm up in a tight grip and holds her high above the ground. Wincing with pain, she kicks at her assailant but to no avail.

With the cadet in tow, Scuzzard walks over to her limping lieutenant and prepares to pound him into the ground with his gigantic foot.

"Just my luck," hisses Scuzzard. "I've come across an all-you-can-eat buffet!"

Chapter 7

From his hiding place, Sideswipe musters up the courage and rushes to the rescue, spiriting Bumblebee away from imminent bashing in the nick of time!

The young Autobot deposits the wounded leader against a thick tree trunk.

"I'm so sorry!" Sideswipe cries. "This is all my fault! I botched the plan!"

"We can't worry about that now," grunts Bumblebee. "I need you to focus on a *new* plan!"

Bumblebee aims the plasma cannon at his wounded leg. He sets the blaster to emit an extremely fine laser beam and mends the gash in his plating.

"Whoa," Sideswipe exclaims. "You *are* a tough-bot, Bee!"

The young Autobot is thoroughly impressed with his sometimes stodgy leader. *Maybe Strongarm is right to look up to him*, he thinks.

"Oh no! Strongarm!"

Sideswipe peeks out from behind a tree to see his teammate struggling in Scuzzard's clutches.

"Time to put my moves to good use again," Sideswipe says.

He jumps onto the nearest tree branch with ninja-like stealth and speed. He zigzags from one to the next until he disappears into the leaves above.

Ignoring his pain, Bumblebee speaks into his communicator.

"Strongarm, what is your status?"

"Oh, I'm just hanging around!" she says gruffly.

"If Strongarm is making jokes, we must *really* be in trouble!" Sideswipe quips.

"Focus, everybot. Sideswipe will be dropping in unexpectedly. Strongarm, disengage!"

"Yes, sir!"

Strongarm shifts into vehicle mode, causing Scuzzard to loosen his grip. She pops her hood, catching him on the beak with the full force of an uppercut.

BAM!

Scuzzard's head snaps back, and he drops the police SUV.

The deranged Decepticon changes into his bird form and flies up into the air. Before he can escape, Sideswipe propels himself from within the treetops and lands on top of Scuzzard.

They spiral back onto the ground, and the Autobot drills Scuzzard beakfirst into the dirt.

Before the Decepticon can recover,

Sideswipe shifts into his vehicle form and drives into Scuzzard, hitting the Decepticon with his bumper and smashing him hard against a tree.

Scuzzard drops to the ground, wheezing and hacking.

Sideswipe is mad at Scuzzard for hurting his friends as well as at himself for putting them in danger. He revs his engine and prepares to strike again. His tires spatter dirt into the air.

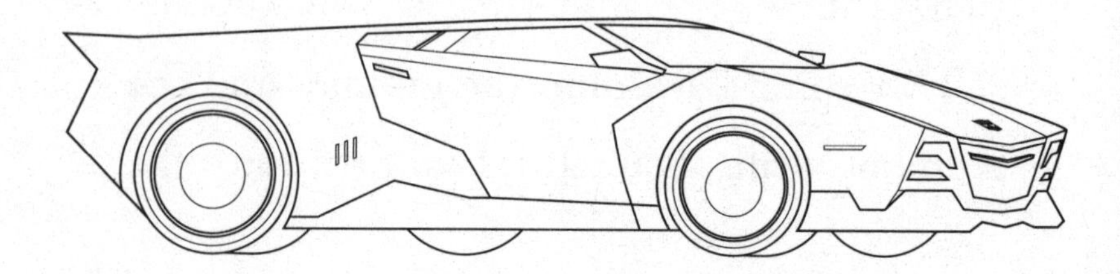

Bumblebee sternly shouts at the red sports car. "Throttle back, Sideswipe. The battle is over."

Sideswipe pulls back and shifts into his bot mode. He stands aside so that Bumblebee and Strongarm, now in bot form, can deploy their neo-forges.

Combining their forces, the heroes trap the Scavengebot in a glowing net of paralyzing energy.

"You mess with Team Bee, you're gonna get stung!" Sideswipe growls.

Scuzzard thrashes against his bonds. "Look at the brave little Autobot now. I've seen how scared you really are."

Sideswipe takes a step back as Bumblebee

and Strongarm tighten their grip on the villain.

"Before this day is done, I am going to feast on all of you!" Scuzzard sneers.

"Ugh, creepy!" Strongarm says with a shudder.

Scuzzard snaps his beak at her.

SNAP!

"Permission to treat the perpetrator as hostile, lieutenant?" she asks Bumblebee.

Before her commanding officer can answer, Strongarm judo-chops the vulture, knocking him out.

KA-POW!

"Wow," Sideswipe says, coming to a slow realization. "Strong. Arm. Now I get it!"

Strongarm lets out an unexpected laugh and quickly regains her composure.

Bumblebee puts his arms around his teammates. “If you want respect, you have to be the first to give it,” he says. “How else will we succeed as a team?”

Sideswipe and Strongarm exchange glances. Their leader is right.

“Let’s get back to the command center,” Bumblebee says.

Back at the scrapyard, Russell and Denny are repairing the pinball machine inside Denny’s garage.

Fixit rolls in and says, “I am very interested in seeing your workstop . . . chop . . . shop!”

"Come in!" Denny says with a big smile. He motions his arm in a grand sweeping gesture. "Welcome to my sanctuary!"

Fixit turns in a complete circle, taking in his new surroundings. There are several benches and shelves completely covered with numerous pieces of hardware and items in various stages of repair.

"It just looks like more of the scrapyard," Fixit says.

"That's what *I* keep telling him," Russell replies.

As Denny tinkers with his tools, he wipes the sweat off his brow.

Fixit focuses his ocular sensors onto Denny's perspiration.

"It appears you are losing fluids, Denny

Clay," Fixit says. "Perhaps one of your pipe valves has sprung a leak?"

Grimlock squeezes his massive frame into the garage.

"We just got word from Bumblebee," the dinobot announces. "They captured the Decepticon! Whoo-hoo!"

Grimlock starts dancing, and the rumbling vibrations rattle the delicate pinball machine. The legs start to wobble and pop off one by one.

"I think there may be one too many dino-bots in my sanctuary," Denny whispers to Russell.

"*Dad*, what am I supposed to do with him?" Russell asks. "It's not like I can take him for a walk or a run at the dog park."

"Exercise is a wonderful idea," Denny says, tousling Russell's hair. "Why don't you practice throwing a few passes? I'm sure Gridlock Grimlock is up for it."

Russell stares at his father, who continues tinkering with the pinball machine.

"Did someone call upon the lob-ball legend?" Fixit asks.

The dinobot perks up. He reconfigures himself into bot mode and cries, "GAME ON!"

Grimlock picks up Fixit in the palm of his hand.

"Release me at once," Fixit demands.

"No, Grimlock," Denny responds with a smile. "I meant you and Rusty could throw around the old pigskin."

“Pigskin!” says Grimlock. “Is that another Decepticon? Let me at ’im!”

“Yes,” begs the beleaguered Fixit. “Throw *him* around for a change!”

“No, no, no,” Russell says, shaking his head. “Pigskin is another term for a football!”

“Ah, yes,” Fixit replies. “The spheroid that is used to play your Earth sport of the same name.”

Grimlock places Fixit back on the ground and bounds out of the workshop. "The legend has returned!"

Denny hugs the pinball machine close and breathes a sigh of relief.

Minutes later, Russell and Grimlock find a clear path in the scrapyard and take turns throwing the football to each other.

Russell rears back and releases the ball, spiraling it through the air at immense speed. Grimlock sprints, pushing his massive robot form to its limit, and dives to catch the football. He snatches the ball out of the air.

Unfortunately, Grimlock's rapid movement makes him an unstoppable force. He lands hard and skids uncontrollably—right into the command center!

SMASH!

CRASH!

Russell watches helplessly as the events seem to unfold in slow motion.

Grimlock bashes into one of the stasis pods, cracking the surface. The chamber tips over and breaks upon impact.

A loud hissing sound comes from within, and a sharp metallic claw scrapes away at the debris. Russell runs as fast as he can to the workshop.

"*Dad!* Fixit!" he yells. "HELP!"

Grimlock groans as he lifts his battered form onto his feet. He turns around to see the shimmering black figure of their old Decepticon nemesis—Filch!

The Corvicon slinks out of the chamber

and stretches her robot limbs while emitting a high-pitched shriek.

"I'M FREE!"

Then she flaps her wings and takes flight.

Grimlock watches the prisoner escape.

"Oh, scrap!" he whispers.

Chapter 8

The trek back to the command center through the forest is long and winding. The Autobots created this path so they could travel unobserved by humans.

Bumblebee, Sideswipe, and Strongarm take turns carrying the unconscious form of Scuzzard. Everybot is lost in thought.

Bumblebee contemplates how the members of this motley crew of his need more field training and how they cannot rely on dumb luck to accomplish their missions.

As if reading Bumblebee's mind, Sideswipe breaks the silence.

"I want to apologize again about what happened back there," the young Autobot says. "I messed things up."

"It's all right, Sideswipe," Bumblebee says. "Any one of us could have gotten lost on this unfamiliar terrain."

"Not only that," Sideswipe says. "I'm mad at myself about being scared and running off. That's not like me. I'm tougher than that. Stronger than that!"

"Toughness is not a sign of strength," Strongarm says.

"Strongarm is right," Bumblebee adds. "You're very good at what you do, and we are all still learning how to work as a team."

Suddenly, a message crackles in through his audio receptors. Bumblebee can barely make out what it is, but he knows it's coming from the command center.

"ZZZK-help-ZZZZK-trouble!"

"Listen up, everybot!" Bumblebee says. "There seems to be a glitch. Let's pick it up and return to base."

As the Autobots charge forward, a dark figure swoops overhead. It screeches loudly as it dive-bombs toward Team Bee.

The Autobots cover their audio receptors, losing their grip on the trussed-up troublemaker.

"SHINY!" Filch squawks, eyeing the metallic sheen of Scuzzard's body.

She digs her talons into his back, and the sharp pain jostles him into consciousness.

"AAAH!" Scuzzard cries.

Filch quickly extends her wings with expert grace and speed, lifting Scuzzard into the air and carrying him away.

The howling Scuzzard hurls insults at his attacker until both fugitives are far beyond the reach of the Autobots.

Sideswipe blinks in disbelief and turns to Strongarm.

"*Sweet solus prime!*" he exclaims. "Was that—"

"Yes," Strongarm replies.

"Did she just—"

"Yes."

"Are we in deep—"

"*Oh* yes."

Bumblebee manages to complete their sentences. "Did our *old* prisoner just fly off with our *new* prisoner?"

"YES!" Strongarm and Sideswipe yell together.

"Scrud!" Bumblebee exclaims.

The Autobots immediately shift from their robot forms into vehicle modes. They race at top speed toward the command center.

"Something must have compromised our home base," Strongarm says. "How else could Filch have escaped her stasis pod?"

"The sooner we get to the bottom of this, the sooner we can settle the score with those slag-heaps," Sideswipe adds. He revs his engine and races past Bumblebee and Strongarm, kicking up a cloud of exhaust and dust.

Bumblebee watches Sideswipe disappear down the hill before them. "Okay, Strongarm, we have to stay calm. What do you remember from our last run-in with Filch?"

"Filch is a Corvicon," Strongarm states. "She has a compulsion to hoard objects with extremely shiny and reflective surfaces. That explains her immediate seizure of Scuzzard. Last time we tussled, she was storing all her stolen goods in the headpiece of the Crown City Colossus. It is unclear where her nest will be at this juncture, or if she has acquired one yet."

"That's why we need to keep our optics wide and be ready for anything," Bumblebee replies.

Finally, the Autobots arrive at the scrapyard and change back into bot mode. Sideswipe is already assessing the devastation inside the command center.

The outer wall has been reduced to a pile of rubble thanks to when Grimlock plowed through it. A cloud of plaster still hangs in the air.

Fortunately, most of the computers and monitors are still up and running, but the communication devices are on the fritz.

Grimlock, Fixit, Russell, and Denny are huddled around the stasis pods. The chamber that once held Filch lies on its side, open and littered with debris.

"I'm such a klutz-o-tron!" Grimlock cries.

"Tell us what happened," Bumblebee says.

Russell recounts the events that transpired earlier, leading up to Filch's escape.

Bumblebee consoles the dinobot.

"It's all right, Grimlock. Let's look at the fuel gauge as half full, shall we?"

He hopes that his positive attitude will be contagious.

"How can I?" Grimlock wails. "This is a massive mistake!"

Denny steps in and tries to lighten the mood. "It just so happens, Fixit has been itching to repair something all day. Maybe this is an opportunity in disguise?"

"Great to hear," Bumblebee says.

"Well, little buddies," Denny says to Fixit and Russell. "The pinball machine can wait."

With his dad, Russell grabs the downed end of the stasis pod and they tilt it back upright. Fixit reconfigures his arm into a hyper-span regulator so that he may begin repairs on the damaged chamber.

Strongarm turns to her team leader and asks, "What's *our* next course of action?"

Bumblebee crosses over to the command center's main console and pulls up the holo-scroll. "Hmm, it appears there are two active Decepticon signals in our vicinity. Must be Scuzzard and Filch."

"They haven't gotten far," Sideswipe says. "If we act fast, we may still catch up to them!"

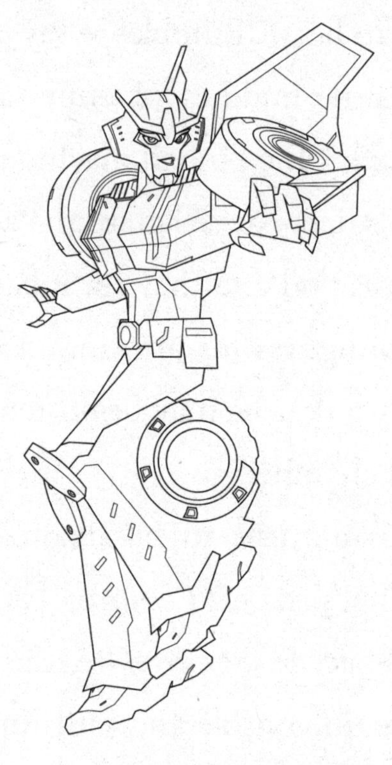

"We *have* to act fast," Strongarm adds. "Or else they'll fly back into the city and put all those civilians at risk."

"Precisely, Strongarm," Bumblebee says. "This time we'll need to combine *all* our forces to take them down."

Grimlock lifts his head with pride as the team leader looks his way.

"Here's the play, Team Bee," Bumblebee commands. "Get out there and cage those birdbots!"

The sun sets over Crown City, and its citizens are unaware of two large winged creatures soaring high above the skyline.

Filch is flying toward the amusement park, attracted by its blinking lights and bright colorful surfaces. She plans to build a new nest atop the Ferris wheel.

"SHINY!" she squeals.

Scuzzard is less enthusiastic.

"Unhand me at once!" he commands.

Filch ignores her captive.

Furious, Scuzzard bites down hard on the Corvicon's foot.

Filch howls and drops the Scavengebot into the empty bumper car pavilion.

SMASH!

Looking around, Scuzzard is pleased with his new surroundings.

"This isn't exactly the central plaza at Kaon, but it definitely deserves a good thrashing," Scuzzard says. "It's hideous!"

He immediately lays waste to the bumper cars. Once they are reduced to scrap, he eats them one by one. His body shimmers and increases in size until he is as big as the pavilion itself!

The Decepticon bursts through the roof of the tent. He looms ominously over the amusement park, casting a dark shadow with his imposing form.

"I'm large and in charge!" Scuzzard cackles.

The Scavengebot sets his sights on the scrumptious skyline of Crown City in the distance.

"Now, *there's* the main course!"

Fearing that her new territory is being threatened, Filch dive-bombs toward Scuzzard. She head butts him in the chest, knocking him off balance.

BAM!

The gigantic robot lurches backward over

the pavilion and crash-lands in the parking lot of Doug's Den.

Seconds later, Scuzzard rises back to his full height. Filch torpedoes toward him once again. The massive monster plucks his flying foe out of the air and crunches her in his grip.

"You won't catch *me* off guard this time, but I'll catch *you*!" he jeers.

At that very moment, Bumblebee and his team of Autobots speed into the parking lot. Grimlock looks up in awe.

"Whoa! Scavengebot versus Corvicon? This is better than Rumbledome!" he shouts.

Scuzzard turns his attention toward the new arrivals and smiles wickedly. "The fun has just begun! Let's play whack-a-bot!"

He stomps and pounds the pavement with

his enormous feet as the heroes scramble to evade being crushed. They swerve and dodge the rapid assault from above, narrowly missing one another.

"Ha! Now I'll get to see some Autobot bumper cars in action!" Scuzzard says with a laugh.

"Your wish is our command sequence!" Sideswipe cries, burning rubber.

He slams right into the Decepticon's foot.

BAM!

"Way to take the lead, Sideswipe," Bumblebee says.

Bumblebee and Strongarm follow their friend and bash into the humongous Decepticon's other foot.

They drive in reverse and then slam into his feet again as if they really are bumper cars!

"Enough games," Scuzzard bellows. "You are nothing but nanodrones to me!"

He hurls Filch at the Autobots, and she lands on top of Bumblebee. The yellow sports car and the Corvicon speed across the parking lot until they come to a screeching halt. Neither of them moves.

Strongarm races to her lieutenant's side.

"Keep that Scavengebot occupied until we can regroup!" she calls out to Sideswipe and Grimlock.

"Hey, birdbrain!" Grimlock shouts at Scuzzard. "I've taken down bigger bots than you with my Dino-Destructo Double Drop!"

"I'd be shocked if that were true," Scuzzard replies. "But I'm willing to let you try. Dinobots make me laugh!"

The Decepticon advances on Grimlock and kneels down to face him.

Sideswipe uses this opportunity to change into his bot mode and springs into action. He sprints toward a nearby lamppost, swings around it with the agility of an acrobat, and leaps onto an adjacent telephone pole. Then he hurls himself off the top and lands right on Scuzzard's back.

"Let's get ready to Rumbledome!" Sideswipe yells.

The flashy Autobot punches the Decepticon right in the head.

POW!

Grimlock follows suit and jumps onto Scuzzard, too.

ROARRR!

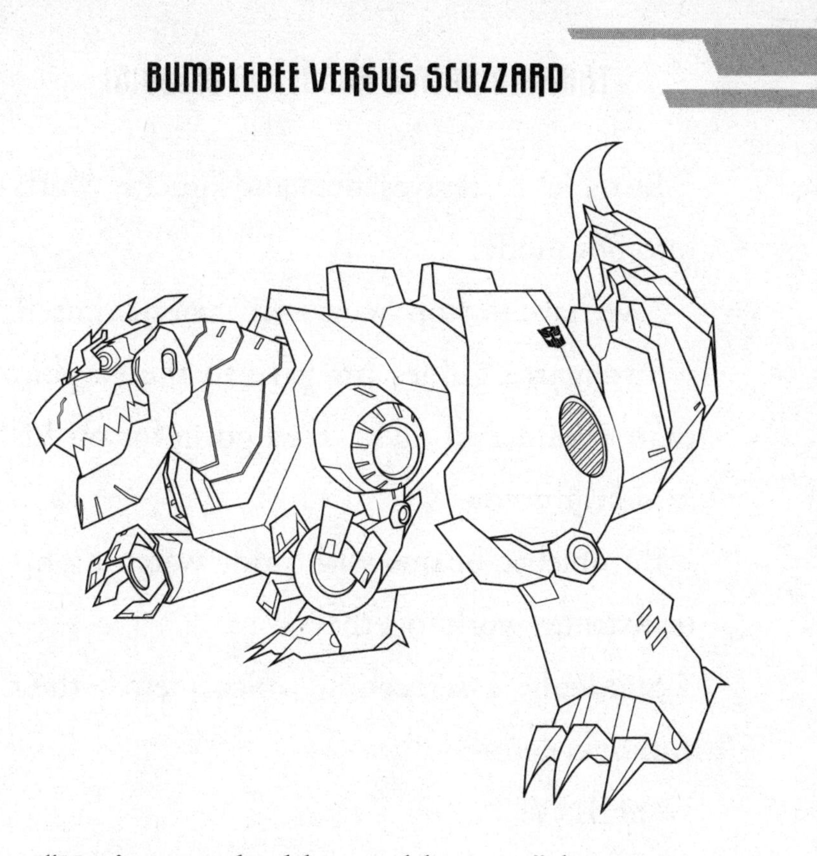

“You’ve got double trouble now!” he quips, and bashes the big robot with his tail.

In the meantime, Strongarm changes into her robot form upon reaching Bumblebee. She pushes Filch off the team leader. The Decepticon twitches and starts to stir.

Bumblebee revives first and quickly shifts into bot mode.

"We have to stop Scuzzard!" he exclaims.

Strongarm guides his gaze to the gargantuan villain and says, "He's got a lot on his mind right now, sir."

Bumblebee beams with pride watching his teammates work together.

Suddenly, a screeching voice pierces their audio receptors.

"SHINY!"

Filch is on her feet and ready to attack.

Bumblebee and Strongarm deploy their neo-forges again and will them to take the shape of an energy staff and crossbow.

Filch charges Bumblebee, pecking at him

with her beak. The Autobot parries with the staff and directs an energy blast at his flying foe.

ZAP!

The Decepticon falls to the ground.

Strongarm shoots an energized grappling hook from her crossbow that loops around Filch's body. The Corvicon hisses and bucks as the glowing rope ties tight.

"We got us a live one here, sir!" Strongarm grunts.

On the other side of the arcade's parking lot, Sideswipe and Grimlock continue to tag-team Scuzzard.

Grimlock throws a jab.

WHACK!

Sideswipe follows with a right hook.

WHAP!

Grimlock lands an uppercut.

WHAM!

Disoriented, the Decepticon flails his arms. One of them catches Grimlock and swats the dinobot onto the pavement.

THUD!

Scuzzard lifts his leg and prepares to make street pizza out of Grimlock.

Sideswipe acts fast and covers the Scavenge-bot's optics with his hands. Scuzzard whirls around blindly while the Autobot guides him toward a telephone pole.

Scuzzard stumbles and his upper body gets tangled in the power lines. Sideswipe swiftly slides down the pole to safety as volts of electricity surge through the wires and overload the Decepticon in a shower of sparks!

ZAAAAAAAARK!

Scuzzard spasms and jolts as he shrinks back to his normal size. Finally, he slumps headfirst into a crumpled, smoldering heap.

BOOM!

"Aw, yeah!" Sideswipe cheers. "Team Bee always brings the buzz!"

Grimlock laughs. "Yeah, he looks a little *shocked*!"

All of a sudden, more electricity crackles behind the duo. They turn to see an illuminated portal light up the night sky.

It is an activated Groundbridge and out from it emerges the bounty hunter and their teammate Drift. "I believe I can be of some assistance," he says.

"Nah, we got everything under control," replies Sideswipe.

Suddenly, someone screams.

"AAAAAAAAH!"

Sideswipe, Grimlock, and Drift turn to see Strongarm hoisted off the ground. She is clutching her crossbow, which is attached to Filch, who is soaring high into the air!

The Corvicon flaps her wings faster and faster, dragging the Autobot along for a wild ride.

Pulling Scuzzard with them, the other three Autobots rush over to their leader.

"What's the plan, Bee?" Sideswipe cries.

"Gridlock Grimlock!" Bumblebee exclaims.

"Reporting for duty," the dinobot calls out.

"Strongarm is going long, and I need you to make the pass," says Bumblebee.

"With what?" Grimlock asks.

"Me."

The plan dawns on the dinobot and he picks up their leader.

Grimlock winds up and snaps Bumblebee into the air. Bumblebee slices through the night sky like a rocket and reaches Strongarm in seconds.

Bumblebee grips her feet, and their combined weight slows Filch down. The trio begins a descent toward the asphalt below.

At that very moment, Doug comes out of the arcade to investigate the commotion behind his store—and is immediately dumbstruck!

He sees Drift and Sideswipe standing over Scuzzard, and Grimlock watching Bumblebee and Strongarm touch down with Filch in tow.

"Scrap!" Sideswipe shouts when he sees the man. "Let's make tracks!"

The young Autobot and the bounty hunter drag Scuzzard into the Groundbridge.

Grimlock helps Bumblebee and Strongarm yank Filch into the portal also before it closes behind them in a blinding flash.

Doug takes off his glasses, rubs his eyes, and puts the glasses back on. He searches the empty parking lot, but the sentient robots have disappeared.

"I must be playing too many video games," he says.

Chapter 10

Team Bee appears at the scrapyard in an instant. The Autobots find themselves behind the tall tower of cars where Grimlock was napping earlier that morning.

Fixit contacts them from the command center.

"Is everybot in one piece?" he asks.

Before they can answer, Filch sees the cars and screeches.

"MORE SHINY!" she squawks.

In a flash, she expands her wings, shoving Bumblebee and Strongarm to the ground. The other Autobots give chase, but the Corvicon is too fast.

Filch flies up to the top of the tower and heaves it with all her might. Tipping and toppling, the cars come crashing down in an avalanche of heavy metal.

"Brace yourselves!" Drift shouts.

With lightning speed, the bounty hunter unsheathes his energy sword and cleaves the first falling car in half. Then he nimbly somersaults out of harm's way.

Bumblebee and the others fire their blasters

at the vehicles, but the onslaught overpowers them.

CHOOM!

CHOOM!

SLAM!

Drift watches in horror as his comrades-in-arms get buried under a pile of used cars. Then he sees Filch heading toward the command center. He is faced with a decision: save his teammates or stop the Decepticon?

Bumblebee emits a muffled cry.

"Drift...help..."

"Jetstorm, Slipstream," he calls out. "Heed your master!"

Jetstorm and Slipstream are Drift's mini-con apprentices who reside upon his armor.

At his command, they hop off and spring into action.

"The captive Corvicon has escaped... again!" announces Drift. "But I must assist my fellow soldiers."

"Of course, master. We're off!"

Jetstorm and Slipstream bow and then zip after Filch. Fixit uploads coordinates directly into their mainframes, instructing them where to guide the Corvicon.

As the mini-cons zigzag through the scrapyard, they scrape their limbs across the metal nearby. The screeching sound and shower of sparks catch Filch's attention.

She hones in on the mini-cons and squeals. "SHINY! For my collection!"

Jetstorm and Slipstream bank left down a crowded aisle. Filch dives after them and chases the mini-cons until they come to a clearing.

And at the end of the aisle, Denny, Russell, and Fixit are waiting for them. They are driving the hydraulic truck!

The two mini-cons split up and zoom in opposite directions, confusing the speeding Corvicon. She flaps her wings to slow down, but it is too late.

Denny activates the magnet and extracts Filch from her flight path straight above!

CLANG!

The Decepticon dangles helplessly while screeching in distress.

"Looks like we're adding you back into *our* collection," Russell replies.

Moments later, the Autobots reconvene at the command center. They look a little worse for wear but are relieved that the Decepticon disaster was finally brought to an end.

Together, they deposit Scuzzard and Filch back into the repaired stasis pods.

"Who says there's no excitement at the scrapyard?" Sideswipe says with a smile.

Russell smiles back and replies, "To be honest, I wouldn't mind some quiet time around here."

"We can always play pinball!" Denny adds with a laugh.

As the group finds itself in a harmonious mood, Bumblebee turns to Drift and says, "Thank you for your assistance today."

"Think nothing of it," Drift says. "It takes a strong Autobot and great leader to ask for help."

"Agreed," Bumblebee nods. He looks at Strongarm, Sideswipe, Fixit, and Grimlock. "There is no problem too big that can't be handled with teamwork," he says.

"And that includes a three-story Decepticon!" Sideswipe adds.

"We accomplished our mission and became better teammates thanks to you, sir," Strongarm says to Bumblebee. "I'm positive Optimus Prime would be very proud."

"Speaking of phenomenal forces," Drift interrupts. "There is indeed a batch of Energon in a quadrant not too far from here. We can set our course for the power source in the morning."

"Awesome," Bumblebee says. "It will definitely give us an advantage in future battles against the Decepticons."

"I agree with you, boss," Grimlock tells his leader. "But don't you think we all deserve to recharge a bit? I know *I* do."

And with that, the dinobot curls up outside the command center and falls fast asleep.

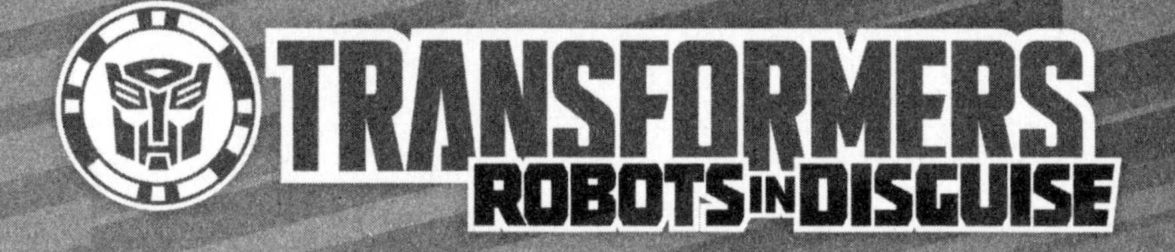

Turn the page for a sneak peek at a new adventure!

Chapter 1

On the outskirts of Crown City, two vehicles are racing on a secluded, miles-long stretch of road. One is a sleek red sports car, zooming far beyond the legal speed limit. The other, trailing behind, is a blue-and-white police cruiser. Both are more than meets the eye. They are really robots in disguise!

The red sports car is Sideswipe, a fast-talking, fun-loving Autobot from the planet Cybertron. Strongarm, the cruiser, is a young cadet from the Cybertronian Police Force. Both Autobots are members of an elite team that keeps Earth safe from a diabolical faction of robots known as Decepticons.

"Aw, yeah!" cheers Sideswipe as the wind rushes past him. "This sure beats sitting around the scrapyard."

"*Slow down!*" orders Strongarm.

The hotheaded Autobot disregards the police-bot's command and picks up more speed. Sideswipe and Strongarm are usually at odds with each other. Sideswipe thinks Strongarm is far too serious and hung up on the rules. Strongarm finds Sideswipe's disregard for order and authority extremely annoying.

The red sports car blasts his radio speakers, filling the air with an earsplitting, guitar-shredding heavy metal song.

"Ack! What an assault on the audio receptors!" Strongarm cries.

"Catch me if you can!" Sideswipe replies. "Or else, eat my dust!"

Sideswipe's tires kick up a cloud of dirt as he barrels faster down the road.

The dust cloud envelops Strongarm, but she does not waver in her course.

"You want to play dirty, Sideswipe? Fine by me," she says. "Eat *this*!"

In an instant, Strongarm shifts from her vehicle mode into her robot form. She somersaults in the air and lands right on top of Sideswipe.

THUD!

"Tag, you're it!" she exclaims.

"Hey, watch the paint job!" Sideswipe cries. "Okay, let's see how *strong* you really are!"

The sports car swerves quickly to the left and then veers hard to the right. Strongarm keeps her grip as well as her cool.

"Is that the best you got?" she taunts. "At the academy, we were taught to expect the unexpected."

"We're making an unexpected stop," Sideswipe says. "And this is where you get off!"

The Autobot slams on his brakes, and his tires squeal against the gravel.

SCREEEEE!

Strongarm hurtles forward and lands on the road in front of Sideswipe.

SLAM!

"Oof!" says Strongarm.

Changing from his vehicle mode into his robot form, Sideswipe lends Strongarm a hand and helps her off the ground.

"Are you okay?" he asks.

"My ego is more bruised than anything else. I should have heeded my own advice."

At that moment, the two Autobots feel a low rumble under their feet. There is another vehicle heading their way.

"Speaking of unexpected, who is that?" Sideswipe asks.

Strongarm focuses her ocular sockets on the approaching object. "It appears to be a human inside a regulation pickup truck. Probably a local produce supplier. Quick, we must maintain our cover!"

In the blink of an eye, Strongarm and Sideswipe change back into vehicles. They idle by the side of the road as the farmer's truck approaches them.

"Too bad," Sideswipe laments. "I was kind of hoping it would be a Decepticon, you know? I'm all revved up and ready for action!"

"Throttle back, tough-bot," Strongarm says.

The two Autobots remain silent as the pickup passes by. The bed of the truck is piled high with crates. Each one is stuffed to the brim with vegetables.

Suddenly, one of the truck's front tires bursts.

BAM!

The driver lets out a cry of alarm as he loses control of the pickup. There is a wrenching sound of metal as the front tires pop off their axis. The crates on the bed of the truck teeter and totter while the vehicle swerves from side to side.

"Whoa!" exclaims Sideswipe. "Who ordered the tossed salad?"

In the distance, another truck is traveling down the same road in the opposite direction.

"Those two vehicles will collide unless we intervene!" Strongarm cries.

"Well, I wanted excitement," Sideswipe replies. "So let's rock and roll!"

TRANSFORMERS
ROBOTS IN DISGU SE
IF YOU LIKE TEAM 'BEE, DON'T MISS OUR COMIC BOOK ADVENTURES EVERY MONTH!
IN PRINT AND DIGITAL, EVERYWHERE COMICS ARE SOLD
idwpublishing.com/transformers
Licensed By:
Hasbro
HASBRO and its logo, TRANSFORMERS and all related characters are trademarks of Hasbro and are used with permission. © 2015 Hasbro. All Rights Reserved. HASBRO and its logo, G.I. JOE and all related characters are trademarks of Hasbro and are used with permission. © 2015 Hasbro. All Rights Reserved.
COMIC SHOP LOCATOR SERVICE
COMICS
888-COMIC-BOO
comicshoplocator.co
idwpublishing.com
idwlimited.com
idwentertainment.com
idwgames.com
IDW®
State of the Art
Facebook: facebook.com/idwpublishi
Twitter: @idwpublishi
tumblr: tumblr.idwpublishing.c
YouTube: youtube.com/idwpublishi
Instagram: instagram.com/idwpublishi
deviantART: idwpublishing.deviantart.c
Pinterest: pinterest.com/idwpublishing/idw-staff-fav